The Window Box Book

written by

KAREN FAUSCH

illustrated by

LAURA JANE COATS

THE LITTLE BOOKROOM

New York

Copyright © 1999 by Karen Fausch
Illustrations Copyright © 1999 by Laura Jane Coats
Design & Art Direction by Angela Hederman
The Little Bookroom acknowledges with appreciation
the contributions of Diane Seltzer, Margarette Devlin,
and Greg Succop and the Woodworkers at the
Little Red School House in New York City.
ISBN 0-9641262-3-0
Library of Congress Catalog Card Number 97-71864
First Printing May 1999

The Little Bookroom

Five Saint Luke's Place, New York
10014
Telephone 212-691-3321
Fax 212-691-2011

Dedication

To Lydia & Her Friends
K. F.

To Sarah & Her Family
L. J. C.

The pages of this book are filled...

WHAT YOU WILL NEED
Page 6

BUILDING A WINDOW BOX
Page 9

OVER THE WINTER
Page 60

THROUGH THE YEAR
Page 64

KEEPING A JOURNAL
Page 65

KEEPING A PLANTING LOG
Page 66

Page 12
Bouquet Box
FLOWERS FOR SUN
Sending a Tussie Mussie

Page 16
Shady Lane Box
FLOWERS FOR SHADE
Creating a Hanging Cone

Page 20
Hungry Rabbit Box
MIXED GREENS
Celebrating with a Salad

Page 24
Candy Box
EDIBLE FLOWERS
Candying Flowers & Flavoring Salads

Page 28
Tea Party Box
HERBS FOR INFUSING
Brewing Chamomile or Sunshine Tea

Page 32
Night & Day Box
BLOSSOMING VINES
Building a Wooden Trellis

with fun & interesting things to do

Page 36

Sweet & Sour Box

CUCUMBERS
Making Pickles

Page 40

Pizza Box

GARLIC & HERBS
Simmering Sauce ❧ Braiding Garlic

Page 44

Jack Be Little Box

MINI PUMPKINS
Painting Jack-o-Lanterns ❧ Carving Initials

Page 48

Everlasting Box

PLANTS FOR DRYING
Arranging Dried Flowers

Page 52

Baby Veggie Box

AUTUMN HARVEST
Serving Crudité and Dip

Page 56

Spring Will Come Box

MINI SPRING BULBS
Filling Tiny Vases ❧ Painting a Still Life

KEEPING A
WATERING LOG
Page 73

ORDERING
SEEDS & BULBS
Page 78

KEEPING A
PURCHASE LOG
Page 79

WINDOW BOX
VISITORS
Page 80

FAVORITE
PLANTS
Page 82

THINGS TO
REMEMBER
Page 86

WINDOW BOX

The plants recommended in this book will grow best in a window box that is about one foot deep. You can build your own window box or buy one. Some of the window boxes sold in stores may be smaller, but they still can accommodate most of the recommended plants, with the exception of cucumbers, pumpkins, and bulbs. Window boxes made of wood, clay, or plastic are best. Metal window boxes tend to get too hot and will cause your plants to overheat.

LOCATION & SAFETY

The best place for a window box is in a sunny location — on a ledge outside your window, or just inside the window. Although most plants prefer at least five hours of direct sunlight each day, many will grow well with less time in direct sunlight if they get reflected or filtered sunlight as well. But don't worry if your window doesn't get a lot of sun. There are a few plants that actually prefer the shade.

If your window box is outside on a ledge, be sure to attach it securely to the building. Even if it is full of soil, a strong wind could blow it over. Not only would you lose your plants, but someone below could be seriously hurt if hit by a falling window box.

DRAINAGE MATERIAL

Line the bottom of your window box with one or two inches of drainage material, such as gravel or perlite. This will help extra water to drain out through the bottom.

POTTING SOIL

Fill your window box to within one inch of the top with potting soil. You can buy a bag of potting soil at the garden center or make your own. To make your own, mix together: 1/3 topsoil, 1/3 compost or peat moss, and 1/3 perlite. Then add one or two cups of dehydrated manure. Mix together and fill your window box to one inch below the top edge.

Seeds & Bulbs

Once you have decided which window box garden to plant first, make a list of the seeds or bulbs you will need. You can buy them at a garden center or purchase them through a mail order catalog. Some seed and bulb companies will even send you free catalogs.

You will have many more seeds in a packet than you need for a window box garden. Share the extras with friends or keep them for next year. Seeds will keep for at least one year if they are stored in an airtight container and kept in a cool, dry, dark place.

Another way to get seeds is to save them from the plants you grow. If you allow the flowers to wither, rather than pick them, seeds or seed pods will form and begin to dry. When they are completely dry collect them in an envelope and label it. Be sure to move quickly when it's time to collect the dry seeds or the birds will beat you to it!

Common names for plants vary from one part of the country to another and are totally different in other languages. In addition to the common names used in the United States, this book gives the botanical names, which are in Latin, and are used throughout the world.

Fertilizer

The best kind of fertilizer to use in your window box garden is a liquid fertilizer called fish emulsion. You can buy it at most garden centers. It contains nitrogen, which is like a vitamin for plants, helping them to grow strong and healthy. Fish emulsion is smelly, but plants love it. The planting instructions in each chapter explain how frequently to fertilize each type of plant. You should also follow the instructions on the container when you use fish emulsion or any other fertilizer.

Watering Can

Before you begin to plant, water the soil thoroughly. After you have planted your seeds water them gently, not only during the days before they have begun to sprout, but also after the seedlings begin to grow. The best way to do this is with a watering can that has a rose tip. The rose tip allows the water to fall lightly in tiny droplets that will not wash away the seeds you have planted or be harmful to small, delicate plants as they begin to grow. If your window box is inside, be sure to put a tray underneath it to collect the excess water as it drains out.

Planting & Germination

Your seeds and bulbs will need just the right combination of moisture, light, and temperature in order to germinate or sprout.

MOISTURE

The soil in your window box should be kept moist for planting seeds. If it dries out, so will your seeds, and then they won't germinate. At the same time it is important not to wash away the seeds with too much water. Bulbs are not as delicate when it comes to watering. They prefer a lightly moist soil that dries out a little between waterings.

LIGHT

All plants need sunlight to grow, but some depend on darkness to germinate or sprout. To protect seeds or bulbs from the light you can temporarily cover your window box with brown paper or newspaper. The planting instructions in each chapter will tell you which seeds and bulbs need to be protected from the light and for how long.

TEMPERATURE

Different seeds and bulbs require different air temperatures to germinate or sprout. The air temperature changes as the seasons change, so planting times must be planned according to the weather. If you plant too early in the year your seeds may not have enough warmth to sprout. If you begin too late your plants may not have enough time to complete their growth cycles before the weather becomes cold again.

The phrases used in the planting instructions for each chapter will help you to know when the temperature is right for planting. *As soon as the soil can be dug* means the soil is no longer frozen and is soft enough to dig. *After frost ends* means the air temperature outdoors at night does not drop below 32° Fahrenheit. *After the soil has warmed* means the air temperature outdoors at night does not drop below 50° Fahrenheit.

Bugs

Insects are sure to visit your window box garden. Some, such as ladybugs, are helpful to plants while others, such as aphids, are not. If you find an insect that you don't recognize, clip off the leaf with the bug on it and put it in a plastic bag. Take it to a garden center or a Cooperative Extension Agent to have it identified. Then ask for advice on what action, if any, you should take to protect your plants.

BUILDING MATERIALS

Pine is one of the most practical materials for building window boxes. *Common White Pine*, also known as *Number 2 Common Pine*, is especially good because it can withstand harsh weather. Redwood and cedar, although more expensive than pine, are also durable. Plywood, however, is not a good choice because moisture will cause it to come apart. Whichever wood you choose, be sure to avoid wood that has been treated with chemicals that carry health warnings.

When you shop for wood you will find that boards come in many sizes. Each is named according to its dimensions. For example, a *One by Twelve* is a piece of wood that is about one inch thick and about twelve inches wide. *One by Twelve* boards are perfect for window boxes and most lumberyards sell them in various lengths.

If you ask at the lumberyard you can select the wood yourself and choose pieces that look nice to you. For a small fee you can also have each piece of wood cut to the correct length. That way you won't need to do any sawing at home.

To build a window box that is 36 inches long, 12 inches wide, and 12 inches deep, like the one shown in this book, you will need to have boards cut to the lengths shown below. You can build your window box with a solid bottom made from a *One by Twelve* board or with four slats made from *One by Two* boards.

A. For the sides: 2 *One by Twelve* pieces, 36 inches long
B. For the ends: 2 *One by Twelve* pieces, 11¼ inches long
C. For the bottom: 1 *One by Twelve* piece, 36 inches long
              or: 4 *One by Two* pieces, 36 inches long

If you make the bottom the window box using four slats you will need to line it with a sheet of plastic screen. This will allow for drainage and prevent soil from falling through the spaces between the slats.

ASSEMBLING THE MATERIALS

Once you have the boards cut to the correct lengths, ask an adult to help you assemble your window box according to the instructions below. You should have (A) two side pieces, (B) two end pieces, and (C) one bottom piece, as shown in Figure 1, or four narrow strips of wood if you are using slats for the bottom of the window box.

To put your window box together, you will need about 40 nails. *6d* or *6-penny* common or finish nails work well.

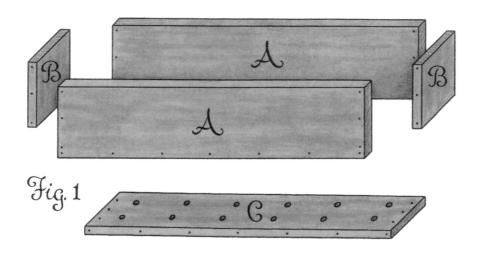

Fig. 1

BUILDING INSTRUCTIONS

1. Position the end pieces (B) between the side pieces (A) with the top edges even, and nail them together. The end pieces should be turned so that the grain runs horizontally.

2. Turn the box upside down, and fit the bottom (C) between the sides and ends, and nail it in place. Then use a drill to make several holes in the bottom of the box for drainage, as shown in Figure 1.

co or co

If you use four *One by Two's* for the bottom of your window box, turn the box upside down and space the four pieces evenly across the bottom. Nail them to the end pieces, then line the inside of the box with a sheet of plastic screen. The screen will allow for drainage and keep the soil from falling through the spaces between the slats.

Your completed window box should look like the diagram in Figure 2.

Finishing & Mounting

Painting or staining your window box will help to prolong the life of the wood and protect it from harsh weather.

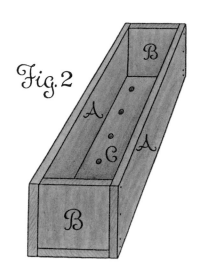

Fig. 2

There are several ways of mounting your window box to the wall or the window ledge. One way is to support it using brackets. Figure 3 shows how *wrought iron brackets* support the window box from below. Figure 4 shows how *L-shaped brackets* support the window box, with the vertical part of the bracket fastened between the side of the box and the wall.

If your window ledge is wide and slanted you can use thick wedges of wood to compensate for the angle so the surface that the window box rests upon will be level, as shown in Figure 5. Begin by fastening the wedges to the window ledge with screws. Then fasten the window box to the wedges, using screws that are long enough to go through the wedges and into the window ledge.

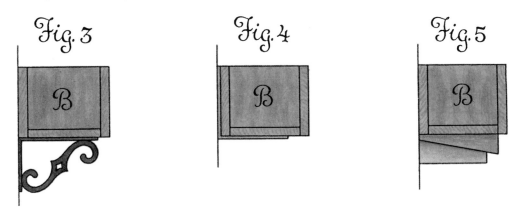

Fig. 3   Fig. 4   Fig. 5

Whichever mounting method you use, be sure to use brackets or wedges that will be strong enough to support the weight of the window box once it has been filled with soil. Fasten the brackets or wedges with strong screws that will hold the box securely in position.

THE
Bouquet Box

FLOWERS FOR SUN

Types to Try

Every flower brings something special to a garden.
The bright colors of marigolds and zinnias will bring butterflies and
snapdragons bring their snap. Just try pinching one!

Zinnia

ZINNIA ~ *Zinnia*

PINWHEEL SERIES grows to be 12 inches tall,
with single flower heads 3½ inches across, in
cherry, orange, rose, salmon, and white.

LOLLIPOP SERIES grows to be 10 inches tall,
with double flower heads 2½ inches across, in
yellow, red, orange, and pink.

Marigold

MARIGOLD ~ *Tagetes*

HAPPY DAYS MIXED grows to be 10 inches tall,
in colored patterns of maroon and gold.

LADIES MIXED or **LADY HYBRID SERIES**
grows to be 20 inches tall with double flower heads
3½ inches across, in yellow, gold, and orange.

Snapdragon

SNAPDRAGON ~ *Antirrhinum*

FLORAL CARPET HYBRID dwarf variety grows
to be 7 inches tall, in pink, yellow, and white.

CINDERELLA MIXED semi-dwarf variety grows
to be 20 inches tall in apricot, pink, and yellow.

DID YOU KNOW?

Flowers have often symbolized certain moods
or emotions. In the *Language of Flowers*, zinnias
mean *'thoughts of absent friends.'*

13

Planting

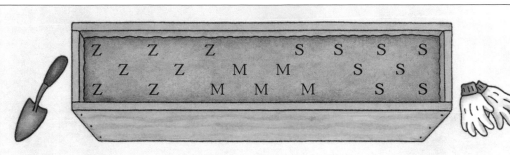

When it's time to plant, follow the diagram above.
The letters in the window box show you where to plant the seeds.

Z is for ZINNIA

Plant after frost ends. The seeds should be 6 to 12 inches apart and 1/4 inch deep. Germination takes 5 to 7 days. Flowers will bloom in summer.

M is for MARIGOLD

Plant after frost ends. The seeds should be 6 to 8 inches apart and 1/4 inch deep. Germination takes 5 to 7 days. Flowers will bloom in summer.

S is for SNAPDRAGON

Plant after the soil has warmed. The seeds should be 6 to 8 inches apart. Press the seeds into the soil but do not cover them. Germination takes 5 to 7 days. Flowers will bloom in summer.

Keep the soil moist. Once your seeds have sprouted and begin to bloom, you can make your garden even more bountiful. If you pinch back new growth at the tips of snapdragons and marigolds, they will branch out. As they grow, more buds will form and you will have even more flowers.

It was once common for people to send messages in the form of bouquets. Each type of flower had a meaning all its own and would convey a different sentiment. What does your tussie mussie have to say?

TUSSIE MUSSIE

To make a tussie mussie you will need:

1 bunch of flowers
1 piece of string
1 small paper doily
1 ribbon, 12 inches long

1. Collect a bunch of flowers from your window box, taking a few from each different kind of plant. Be sure to leave a long stem on each flower when you cut it.

2. Cut a small circle in the center of the paper doily. It should be large enough for the stems of your flowers to fit through.

3. Arrange your flowers to make a nice bouquet, then loosely tie the stems together at the top with a piece of string.

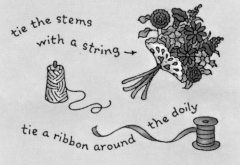

4. Put the stems through the hole in the paper doily and fold the edges of it up around the flowers.

5. Now tie the ribbon around the center of the doily, close to where the stems come through.

6. Your tussie mussie is now ready to deliver to a favorite person.

THE
Shady Lane Box

FLOWERS FOR SHADE

Types to Try

Some plants prefer the shady side of the street, where eveything seems a little cooler and a little quieter. A shade garden will brighten your window box with colorful leaves and flowers.

BROWALLIA ~ *Browallia speciosa*

BLUE BELLS IMPROVED grows to be 10 to 14 inches tall with star-shaped blue flowers.

SILVER BELLS grows to be 10 to 14 inches tall with star-shaped white flowers.

TORENIA ~ *Torenia*

PANDA PINK grows to be 4 inches tall and has white flowers with rose pink markings at the edges.

CLOWN MIXED grows to be 8 inches tall and has flowers in a range of deep velvety colors.

COLEUS ~ *Coleus x hybridus*

WIZARD MIXED grows to be 10 inches tall and has heart-shaped leaves in red, pink, and apricot with cream or green markings at the edges.

SABER MIXED grows to be 8 to 12 inches tall and has long sword-like leaves with patterns of green and rose or green and white.

BALSAM ~ *Impatiens balsamia*

SUGAR or CANDY MIXED dwarf variety grows to be 10 inches tall and has double rose-shaped flowers in shades of pink, rose, and white.

Planting

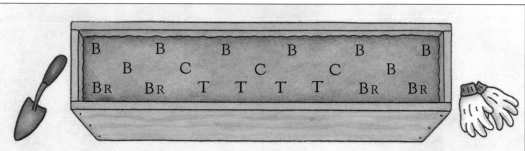

When it's time to plant, follow the diagram above.
The letters in the window box show you where to plant the seeds.

BR is for BROWALLIA

Start indoors, planting seeds 6 inches apart. Press seeds into the soil but do not cover them. Transfer seedlings to the window box after the soil has warmed. Germination takes 14 to 21 days.

T is for TORENIA

Start indoors, planting seeds 6 inches apart and 1/8 inch deep. Transfer seedlings to the window box after the soil has warmed. Germination takes 15 to 20 days.

C is for COLEUS

Plant after the soil has warmed. Seeds should be 8 inches apart and 1/4 inch deep. Press seeds into the soil but do not cover them. Germination takes 15 to 20 days.

B is for BALSAM

Plant after the soil has warmed. Seeds should be 8 to 10 inches apart and 1/16 inch deep. Germination takes 10 to 15 days.

These flowers will bloom all summer and into
the fall. The coleus will branch out and grow more leaves
if you pinch back new growth at the tips.

One Good Turn

Do you have a friend who needs cheering up?
Hang a cone filled with brightly colored flowers on the doorknob.
When your friend opens the door, a surprise will be waiting.

HANGING CONE

To create a hanging cone you will need:

> 1 sheet of construction paper
> 1 bunch of flowers
> Stickers or colored markers

1. Cut a one inch-strip from the long edge of the construction paper.

2. Cut a large half-circle from the remaining piece of paper.

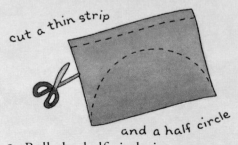

cut a thin strip

and a half circle

3. Roll the half-circle into a cone, overlapping the edges. Use glue or tape it to hold it in position.

4. Decorate the paper cone using stickers or colored markers.

roll the paper into a cone

form a loop handle

5. Form a loop out of the long strip of paper and staple the ends of it to the top edge of the cone.

6. Collect flowers from the window box and arrange them in the paper cone.

surprise someone!

7. Hang your cone full of flowers on a friend's front door for a happy surprise!

THE Hungry Rabbit Box

MIXED GREENS

Types to Try

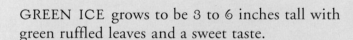

Nothing makes a rabbit happier than nibbling on fresh lettuce. It will make you happy, too. Dark green arugula mixed with light green and red lettuces will create a colorful salad.

ARUGULA ~ *Eruca vesicaria sativa*

ROQUETTE grows to be 3 to 5 inches tall with smooth dark green leaves. It has a peppery flavor that will add zip to your salad.

LOOSELEAF LETTUCE ~ *Lactuca sativa*

MIGHTY RED OAK grows to be 3 to 6 inches tall and has burgundy colored leaves similar to those of an oak tree.

GREEN ICE grows to be 3 to 6 inches tall with green ruffled leaves and a sweet taste.

GOURMET BLEND grows to be 3 to 6 inches tall and includes five different kinds of lettuce. Each adds its own shape and color to the mix.

DID YOU KNOW?

Gardeners have always planted seeds according to the calendar. Before modern calendars, people relied on the sun and moon to be their guides.

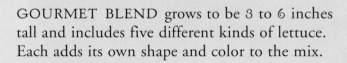

21

Planting

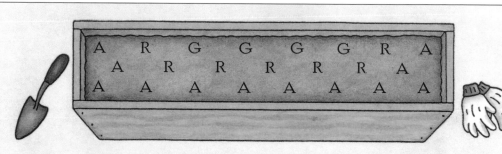

When it's time to plant, follow the diagram above.
The letters in the window box show you where to plant the seeds.

A is for ARUGULA

Plant as soon as the soil can be dug. For fall growing, plant in early August. Seeds should be 4 to 6 inches apart and 1/2 inch deep. Germination takes 7 days. Leaves will be ready to eat in 35 days.

R is for RED OAK

Plant as soon as the soil can be dug. For fall growing, plant in early August. Seeds should be 4 to 6 inches apart. Press seeds into the soil but do not cover them. Germination takes 7 to 10 days. Leaves will be ready to eat in 45 to 50 days.

G is for GREEN ICE or GOURMET BLEND

Plant as soon as the soil can be dug. For fall growing, plant in early August. Seeds should be 4 to 6 inches apart. Press seeds into the soil but do not cover them. Germination takes 7 to 10 days. Leaves will be ready to eat in 45 to 50 days.

Keep well watered. Fertilize the soil once before planting and then once again after three weeks.

Perfect for Peter

When the leaves of your plants look big enough to eat, pinch them off an inch above the soil. Or you can pull them up, roots and all, if you're ready to plant something new.

CELEBRATING SALAD

To make a salad you will need:

Lettuce and arugula leaves

1. Pick some leaves from each of the different types of plants in your window box. That way your salad will have a variety of colors, tastes, and textures.

wash the leaves

2. Wash the leaves gently in cold water and dry them, using a salad spinner if you have one. If not, shake the leaves lightly and spread them on a towel to dry.

3. If you decide not to make your salad right away, store the leaves in a plastic bag in the refrigerator until you are ready to use them.

add cucumbers, carrots

tomatoes and olives

4. Gently mix the leaves together in a large bowl, and add chopped carrots, tomatoes, or cucumbers, or whatever you like. Be creative. What would taste good in a salad?

5. Invite someone to share your salad, and celebrate your harvest.

SALAD DRESSING

You can make a salad taste sweet or tangy with different types of dressing. On page 62 is a recipe for vinegar and oil dressing.

The Candy Box

EDIBLE FLOWERS

Types to Try

Pansies, nasturtiums, and lemon marigolds are as bright and colorful as candy, and the best part is that their flowers are actually edible. You can even eat the leaves of your nasturtiums.

Nasturtium

NASTURTIUM ~ *Tropaeolum*

DOUBLE DWARF JEWEL SERIES grows to be 12 inches tall with double flowers in gold, mahogany, rose, and yellow.

WHIRLYBIRD grows to be 12 inches tall with semi-double flowers in seven colors: cherry rose, gold, mahogany, orange, scarlet, tangerine, and cream.

Pansy

PANSY ~ *Viola*

MAXIMUM HYBRID MIXED grows to be 6 to 8 inches tall with 1- to 2-inch flower heads in blue, orange, red, yellow, and white.

JOHNNY JUMP-UP grows to be 6 to 8 inches tall with 1- to 1½-inch flower heads in blue, orange, red, yellow, and white.

Marigold

LEMON MARIGOLD ~ *Tagetes signata pumila*

SIGNET GEM grows to be 8 inches tall with 1- to 1½-inch single flower heads in yellow and orange.

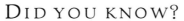

DID YOU KNOW?

RABBIT TALES

Birds plant lots of seeds, even if they don't intend to. If a bird drops a seed it is carrying, it may sprout and grow wherever it lands.

25

Planting

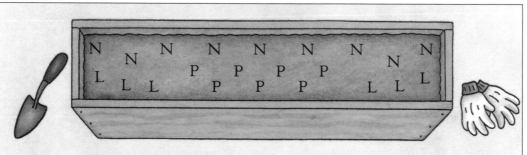

When it's time to plant, follow the diagram above.
The letters in the window box show you where to plant the seeds.

N is for NASTURTIUM

Plant after frost ends. Seeds should be 8 inches apart and 1/4 inch deep. They need darkness to germinate. After planting, cover the seeds with brown paper or newspaper for 7 to 12 days, until they have germinated. Then remove the paper. The flowers will bloom in summer and fall.

P is for PANSY

Plant as soon as the soil can be dug. Seeds should be 6 inches apart and 1/8 inch deep. Germination takes 10 to 21 days. The flowers will bloom in spring and die back during the summer. If left in the window box, they may bloom again in the fall.

L is for LEMON MARIGOLD

Plant as soon as the soil can be dug. Seeds should be 6 inches apart and 1/16 inch deep. Germination takes 5 to 14 days. The flowers will bloom in summer and fall.

Remember to keep the soil moist.
Do not use fertilizer.

Real nasturtiums or pansies look much lovelier on a cake than flowers made out of icing. Dress up your desserts with just-picked blossoms or candy them for added sweetness.

CANDIED FLOWERS

To make candied flowers you will need:

1 cup of pansies or marigolds
Pasteurized egg whites
1 cup of sugar

1. Collect some flowers from your window box and trim off the stems.

2. Line a baking sheet or a tray with waxed paper and arrange the flowers in rows, one inch apart.

3. Beat the egg whites with a whisk until they become frothy and then paint the egg whites onto the flowers using a small brush.

4. Sprinkle the flowers with sugar, or use tweezers to dip them into a bowl of sugar, coating both sides of each flower.

5. Set the tray of flowers in a cool place until they are completely dry. Then use them to decorate desserts.

FLOWERS FOR SALADS

Some types of flowers are poisonous. Always ask an adult if a flower is edible before you taste it. Turn to page 62 to find a salad recipe that uses edible flowers.

THE
Tea Party Box

HERBS FOR INFUSING

Types to Try

Mint tastes and smells refreshing. On a hot afternoon, pop a mint leaf into your mouth, or make a tall, cool glass of mint iced tea. Chamomile and lemon balm make good tea, too.

MINT ~ *Mentha*

PEPPERMINT grows to be 2 feet tall with dark purple stems and lavender flower spikes.

SPEARMINT grows to be 2 feet tall with lilac-colored flowers, and is milder than peppermint.

CHOCOLATE MINT grows to be 1 foot tall and has chocolate-colored stems, pale pink flower spikes, and a chocolate flavor.

PINEAPPLE MINT grows to be 1 to 1½ feet tall and has green leaves with creamy edges, white flower spikes, and a fruity scent and flavor.

APPLE MINT grows to be 1 to 2 feet tall and has soft, velvety leaves, blue and white flower spikes, and an apple-like scent and flavor.

CHAMOMILE ~ *Matricaria recutita*

GERMAN CHAMOMILE grows to be 12 to 20 inches tall and has ferny gray-green leaves and daisy-like white flowers with yellow centers.

LEMON BALM ~ *Melissa officinalis*

COMMON LEMON BALM grows to be 2 to 3 feet high and has green, heart-shaped leaves with a lemony flavor and scent.

Planting

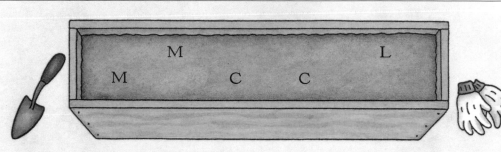

When it's time to plant, follow the diagram above.
The letters in the window box show you where to plant the seeds.

M is for MINT

Plant after the soil has warmed. Seeds should be 12 inches apart and 1/4 inch deep. Germination takes 12 to 16 days. Leaves can be eaten at any time or can be dried to use later.

C is for CHAMOMILE

Plant after the soil has warmed. The seeds should be 6 to 12 inches apart. Press seeds into the soil but do not cover them. Germination takes 10 to 21 days. Flowers bloom in summer and then can be picked for making tea.

L is for LEMON BALM

Plant as soon as the soil can be dug. The seeds should be 12 inches apart and 1/8 inch deep. Germination takes 14 days. Leaves can be eaten at any time or can be dried to use later.

To dry mint or lemon balm leaves tie
the stems together and hang them upside down in
a dry spot, away from direct sunlight.

Put the Kettle On

Tea is good, hot or cold. For more flavor, squeeze a touch of lemon into mint tea. Sweeten lemon balm tea with a spoonful of honey, or add a cinnamon stick to chamomile tea while it's steeping.

CHAMOMILE TEA

To make chamomile tea you will need:

5 to 6 flower heads for each cup

1. After your chamomile flowers have bloomed and the petals have dropped off, pick several flower heads, leaving the stems long.

2. Tie the stems together and hang them upside down to dry.

pick flower heads

hang upside down

3. When the flower heads are dry, you can store them in a tin.

4. To brew a cup of tea, place 5 or 6 flower heads in a tea strainer.

5. Put the tea strainer in a cup of hot water and allow the tea to steep until it is lightly flavored.

relax with a cup of tea

6. Now find a cozy spot, open your favorite book, and sip a nice cup of tea at the end of your busy day. Chamomile tea has a mild sedative quality, which means that it can help you to feel calm and relaxed.

SUNSHINE TEA

You can make sunshine tea from mint or lemon balm leaves, but you will need plenty of sunshine. Turn to page 62 for a recipe.

The
Night & Day Box

BLOSSOMING VINES

Types to Try

Morning glories open gloriously at dawn, but they usually fade by noon. However, you can then look forward to the moonflowers, which bloom at dusk and stay open all night.

Heavenly Blue

Moonflower

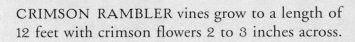
Crimson Rambler

MORNING GLORY ~ *Ipomoea tricolor*

HEAVENLY BLUE vines grow to a length of 8 feet with heart-shaped leaves and sky-blue flowers opening 5 inches across.

CRIMSON RAMBLER vines grow to a length of 12 feet with crimson flowers 2 to 3 inches across.

SCARLET O'HARA vines grow to a length of 8 feet with vivid red blossoms.

TALL MIX vines grow to a length of 12 feet with blue, scarlet, white, and lavender flowers.

MOONFLOWER ~ *Calonyction* or *Pomoea alba*

GIANT WHITE vines grow to be 15 feet long and have white flowers 6 inches across with a lovely fragrance.

DID YOU KNOW?

To watch a moonflower open, you will have to be quick ～ the petals unfold in less than a minute.

Planting

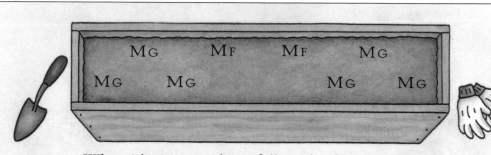

When it's time to plant, follow the diagram above.
The letters in the window box show you where to plant the seeds.

MG is for MORNING GLORY

MF is for MOONFLOWER

Plant morning glories and moonflowers after frost ends.
Soak the seeds in warm water for 1 to 2 days before planting
to speed germination. Plant the seeds 6 to 12 inches apart
and 1/4 to 1/2 inch deep. Keep the soil moist but do not
fertilize. Germination takes 8 to 10 days. Flowers will
bloom in summer and fall.

Morning glory and moonflower vines tend to grow quite
long. Follow the instructions on page 35 to build a
trellis for them.

Some gardens are designed to be enjoyed in
the evening and are called moon gardens. They usually include
flowers that open at dusk. The plants often have a
perfume-like fragrance. White flowers are a popular
choice for moon gardens because they reflect light,
making them easy to see in moonlight.

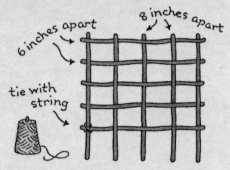

Vines love to climb. They will wrap their tendrils around anything that's handy. A trellis gives the flowers something to cling to. Your pumpkins and cucumbers will like it, too.

BUILDING A TRELLIS

To make a trellis you will need:

10 wooden stakes or thin branches ¼ to ½ inch thick and 3 feet long
1 ball of string

1. Arrange five stakes on the floor eight inches apart. These will be the vertical stakes.

6 inches apart

8 inches apart

tie with string

2. Now arrange the remaining five stakes horizontally about six inches apart. The bottom stake will be about ten inches above the lower end of the vertical stakes.

3. Now weave the horizontal stakes over and under the vertical stakes, alternating on each row.

4. Wrap a piece of string around each place where the stakes cross and tie it tightly.

insert stakes into soil

5. Insert the vertical stakes about eight inches into the soil of your window box. You may also want to attach the upper corners to the wall.

The
Sweet & Sour Box

CUCUMBERS

Cucumbers fresh from the garden are very cool and they're not just for eating. Try closing your tired eyes, then place a slice of cucumber over each one for a refreshing break.

CUCUMBER ~ *Cucumis sativus*

PICKLEBUSH Vines grow to a length of 2 feet with $4\frac{1}{2}$-inch cucumbers.

CORNICHON mini-French pickle vines grow to a length of 2 feet with 2- to 3-inch cucumbers.

SALAD BUSH HYBRID vines grow to a length of 15 inches with 5- to 6-inch cucumbers.

FANFARE HYBRID vines grow to a length of $2\frac{1}{2}$ feet with 8-inch dark-green cucumbers.

NOTE:
Cucumbers will be ready to eat in 50-55 days.

DID YOU KNOW?

Cucumbers can be enjoyed all year, not just at harvest time. The trick is to preserve them in jars. It's a great way to turn a cucumber into a pickle.

37

Planting

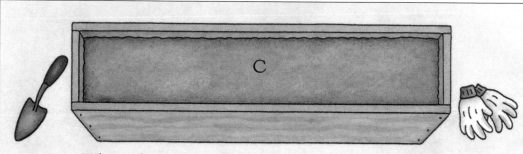

When it's time to plant, follow the diagram above.
The letter in the window box shows where your cucumber plant
will be after you have thinned the seedlings.

C is for CUCUMBER

Plant three seeds one inch apart a week or two after frost
ends. Plant the seeds 1/2 inch deep. Germination takes 7 to
10 days. After germination, thin the seedlings, leaving only
the largest plant.

Because cucumbers require large amounts of water and
nutrients it is best to grow just one vine in a window box.

Cucumber vines tend to grow quite long so you may want
to provide them with a trellis. If you've built the trellis
shown on page 35 for morning glories and moonflowers
you can use it for your cucumbers as well.

Cucumber plants need to have a sunny
site with at least six hours of direct sunlight each day. Keep
the soil moist and fertilize once before planting
and then every three weeks.

Pickles are perfect for picnics. Whether you prefer yours sweet and crisp or mouth-puckering and sour, always pack your picnic basket with a jar of home-made pickles.

SOUR PICKLES

To make sour pickles you will need:

1 quart-size container with a lid

5 cups cucumbers, sliced in half lengthwise

$1/2$ to 1 tablespoon mustard seeds

1 clove of garlic, flattened

$1/2$ to 1 teaspoon whole black peppercorns

5 large sprigs fresh dill

1 quart water

$1/8$ cup white vinegar

$1/8$ cup Kosher salt

1. Place the cucumbers, mustard seeds, garlic, peppercorns, and dill in the container, leaving at least $1/2$ inch of space at the top.

2. Bring the water, vinegar, and salt to a boil in a saucepan and then continue boiling for two to three minutes.

3. Pour the mixture into the jar until it covers the cucumbers.

4. Allow the jar to cool to room temperature, then refrigerate it.

5. Eat your pickles the next day, or save them for a picnic. The longer you wait, the stronger the flavor will be. They will keep for up to two weeks in the refrigerator.

If you prefer your pickles sweet, follow the recipe on page 63.

THE
Pizza Box

GARLIC & HERBS

Types to Try

Basil, oregano, and garlic are among the most frequently used herbs in Italian cooking and they can all be grown easily in a window box.

OREGANO ~ *Origanum*

WILD OREGANO grows to be 1 to 2 feet tall and is a perennial herb which may live through the winter in your window box.

SWEET MARJORAM is an annual with small wooly leaves that grows to be 8 to 12 inches tall and is thought to have the best flavor among plants in the oregano family.

GARLIC ~ *Alium tuberosum*

ROCAMBOLE, unlike other varieties, is a type of garlic that can be planted in the spring.

BASIL ~ *Ocimum basilicum*

DWARF BUSH FINELEAF grows to be 12 inches tall with 1-inch green leaves.

SWEET BASIL grows to be 2 feet tall with 1- to 2-inch oval-shaped leaves.

DID YOU KNOW?

Certain plants require a gentle touch. Basil leaves, for example, bruise easily. Black spots will appear if the leaves are handled too much after picking.

Planting

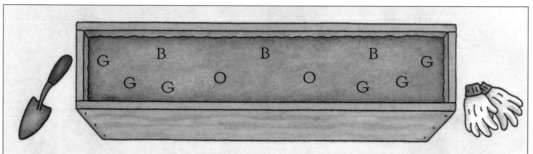

When it's time to plant, follow the diagram above. The letters in the window box show where to plant the seeds and bulbs.

O is for OREGANO

Plant after the soil has warmed. Seeds should be 10 inches apart and 1/8 inch deep. Germination takes 8 to 21 days. Leaves will be ready to harvest in summer and autumn.

G is for GARLIC

Plant bulbs in spring after the soil has warmed. Separate bulbs into individual cloves, discarding any that feel soft. Leave the paper-like skin on. Plant 5 inches apart and 2 inches deep with pointed ends up. For spring planting, harvest garlic in autumn when leaves turn yellow.

B is for BASIL

Plant after the soil has warmed. Seeds should be 10 inches apart and 1/16 to 1/4 inch deep. Germination takes 7 to 21 days. Leaves will be ready to harvest in summer and autumn.

Keep the soil evenly moist,
but don't overwater. Fertilize with liquid
fertilizer once a month.

To Top Things Off

Plan a pizza party and use your herbs to make the sauce below. Your friends are bound to ask for seconds so you may want to double the recipe.

PIZZA OR PASTA SAUCE

To make sauce you will need:

1 clove garlic, minced
1/4 cup chopped onion
1 tablespoon olive oil
2 fresh plum tomatoes, chopped
15-ounce can tomato sauce
1 tablespoon oregano, chopped
1 tablespoon basil, chopped
1/2 teaspoon wine vinegar
1/2 teaspoon sugar
Salt & pepper to taste

sauté onion and garlic

1. Sauté the garlic and onion in olive oil until soft.

2. Add the fresh tomatoes and stir for one to two minutes.

3. Add the tomato sauce, oregano, basil, vinegar, sugar, salt, and pepper and cook over low heat for ten minutes.

pour over pasta   top off a pizza

4. Pour the sauce over pasta or use it as a topping on your pizza.

GARLIC SPROUTS

Clip the green sprouts from one of your garlic plants, then chop them and sprinkle on a salad or a sandwich. Unlike garlic bulbs, the sprouts have a mild flavor.

GARLIC BRAIDS

Making garlic braids is another fun thing you can do with garlic. The instructions are on page 63.

THE Jack Be Little Box

MINI PUMPKINS

Types to Try

Apumpkin patch in a window box? Yes, it can be done!
All that is needed is a window box that is 12 inches deep, six or more
hours of sunlight each day, and plenty of water in hot weather.

PUMPKIN ~ *Cucurbita pepo*

SPOOKTACULAR grows orange pumpkins that
are 6 inches across and ripen in 90 days.

BABY BOO grows white pumpkins that are 3
inches across and ripen in 95 days.

MUNCHKIN MINI grows orange pumpkins that
are 3 inches across and ripen in 80 days.

JACK-BE-LITTLE grows orange pumpkins that
are 6 inches across and ripen in 95 days.

BABY BEAR grows orange pumpkins that are 6
inches across and ripen in 105 days.

Planting

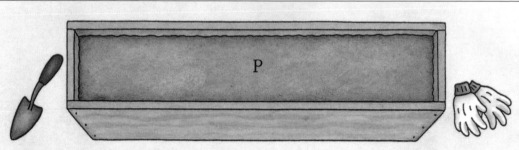

P

When it's time to plant, follow the diagram above. The letter in the window box shows where to plant the seeds.

P is for PUMPKIN

After frost ends, plant three seeds about one inch deep. Germination take about 7 to 10 days. After germination, thin the seedlings, leaving only the largest plant.

Because pumpkin plants require large amounts of water and nutrients, it is best to grow only one vine in a window box.

Fertilize the soil once before planting and then again every three weeks. Pumpkins need full sun. Keep well watered.

Pumpkins will be ready to eat or decorate in 80 to 105 days.

Pumpkins vines can become quite long so you may want to provide them with a trellis. See page 35 for how to build a trellis.

Making Faces

Sow the seeds in spring, and you'll have pumpkins for Halloween. Will you paint scary faces on them? Make a pumpkin pie? Whatever you decide, happy haunting!

PAINT A PUMPKIN

To paint a pumpkin you will need:

Markers or tempera paints
Mini pumpkins

1. Select a pumpkin from your window box and cut the stem.

2. Decide what sort of face you want your pumpkin to have. Make it silly, sad, or scary. It's up to you.

3. Use colored markers or tempera paints to give your pumpkin a face. Small brushes are best for painting pumpkins. If you make a mistake, you can wipe it off and start again.

CARVE YOUR INITIALS

To carve your initials you will need:

A very small pumpkin, still on the vine
A knife with a pointed tip

1. While your pumpkins are still very small, select one you can reach easily, but leave it on the vine.

2. Ask an adult to help you carve your initials or a small design on the pumpkin, using the tip of the knife. Carve the marks very lightly so that they just scratch the skin of the pumpkin and be careful not to break the stem as you are carving.

3. As your pumpkin grows, you will see your initials growing, too.

The Everlasting Box

PLANTS FOR DRYING

Types to Try

Growing everlasting plants is like having a bank account in a window box. But instead of saving money, you save plants. These plants can be dried and saved for long-lasting beauty.

CHINESE LANTERN ~ *Physalis alkekengi*

CHINESE LANTERN grows to be 2 feet tall with bright orange seed pods 2 inches across that look like miniature lanterns.

MONEY PLANT ~ *Lunaria annua*

MONEY PLANT grows to be 30 inches tall and has lavender flowers followed by silvery disk-shaped seed pods 2 inches across.

STATICE ~ *Limonium sinuatum*

PETITE BOUQUET MIX grows to be 12 inches tall and has tiny clusters of flowers in rose, white, yellow, or blue.

DID YOU KNOW?

A seed has an incredible memory. It stores the instructions on when to sprout, when to bloom, its size, color, and shape — all in one tiny seed.

Planting

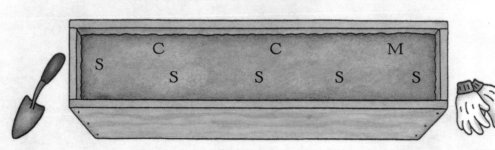

When it's time to plant, follow the diagram above.
The letters in the window box show you where to plant the seeds.

C is for CHINESE LANTERN

Plant as soon as the soil can be dug. The seeds should be 12 to 15 inches apart. Press the seeds into the soil but do not cover them. Germination takes 20 to 25 days. Flowers will bloom in summer, followed by orange seed pods in autumn.

M is for MONEY PLANT

Plant as soon as the soil can be dug. The seeds should be 12 to 15 inches apart and 1/8 inch deep. Germination takes 10 to 14 days. Flowers will bloom in summer, followed by silvery seed pods in autumn.

S is for STATICE

Plant after frost ends. The seeds should be 12 inches apart and just barely covered with soil. Germination takes 10 to 20 days. Flowers will bloom in summer.

These plants will do well if your window box gets
at least five hours of direct sunlight each day. Take care
not to overwater. Do not use fertilizer.

Have you ever wished you could keep your flowers forever?
Plant everlastings, and you can. Dry the flowers or seed pods and you
can make arrangements that will last for a very long time.

DRYING FLOWERS

To make dried flowers you will need:

> *Chinese lanterns, statice,*
> *and money plant*
> *A wide-mouth jar or a can*

1. Collect flowers from your statice plants and seed pods from your money plants and Chinese lanterns by cutting each one close to its base, leaving a long stem.

2. Remove the leaves.

3. To dry statice, tie three to five stems together and hang them upside down in a dry spot, away from direct sunlight.

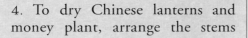

4. To dry Chinese lanterns and money plant, arrange the stems loosely in a jar or can and place it in a dry spot, away from direct sunlight.

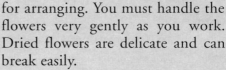

5. When the stems of the plants feel brittle, your dried flowers are ready for arranging. You must handle the flowers very gently as you work. Dried flowers are delicate and can break easily.

GIFTS & DECORATIONS

A dried flower arrangement can make a pretty table decoration. Create a lasting gift by arranging flowers in a basket and adding a colorful ribbon to the handle. Turn to page 63 for instructions on how to make a gift basket.

THE BabyVeggieBox

AUTUMN HARVEST

Types to Try

If you live in a neighborhood with lots of rabbits, beware! They can devour entire rows of carrots and radishes. Luckily, window boxes are usually out of reach, even for rabbits who jump.

CARROT. ~ *Daucus carota sativus*

THUMBELINA carrots are round and are ready to harvest when they are about the size of golf balls.

SHORT & SWEET carrots are oblong and are ready to harvest when they are 4 inches in length.

RADISH ~ *Raphanus sativus*

CHERRY BOMB radishes are red and grow to be $1^1/_2$ inches around. They have a spicy flavor.

EASTER EGG radishes are oval-shaped and grow to be $1^1/_2$ inches around in shades of pink, red, and white.

BURPEE WHITE radishes grow to be 1 inch across. The root is white, crisp, and has a mild flavor.

Planting

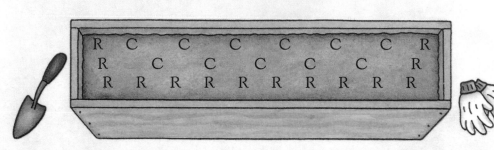

When it's time to plant, follow the diagram above.
The letters in the window box show you where to plant the seeds.

C is for CARROT

For an autumn harvest, plant seeds in mid-August. For a spring harvest, plant as soon as the soil can be dug. Seeds should be 1/2 inch deep. Germination takes 14 to 21 days. After the seeds sprout, thin the seedlings to 2 inches apart. Carrots will be ready to eat in 60 to 70 days.

To keep your carrots from turning green, replace any soil that washes away around their tops.

R is for RADISH

To plant radishes follow the instructions given above for carrots. Germination takes 4 to 6 days. They will be ready to eat in 25 days.

Because radishes grow in about half the time it takes to grow carrots, you can grow two crops of radishes for every one crop of carrots. Or you can plant the radishes 3 or 4 weeks after planting the carrots.

Carrots and radishes need full sun.
Fertilize once before planting and then again every
two weeks. Keep the soil moist.

Your baby veggies look too cute to eat, but you
will be glad if you do. Nothing will compare with the delicious crunch
of a carrot or a radish picked from your own window box.

CRUDITÉ & DIP

To make crudité and dip you will
need:

> Carrots and radishes
> 1 large package of cream cheese
> $1/4$ cup plain yogurt
> 1 to 2 tablespoons fresh herbs

1. When your carrots and radishes
are at least one inch in diameter,
pull them out of the soil.

2. Wash them well in cold water
and trim off the greens.

wash carrots and radishes

trim off green tops

3. Now you have crudité, which is
the French word for raw vegetables.

4. To make dip for your vegetables,
put the yogurt and cream cheese
together in a bowl and mix them.

basil, dill and chives

cream cheese and yogurt

5. Finely chop the fresh herbs and
mix them together in the bowl with
the yogurt and cream cheese.

arrange crudité and dip on a platter

and eat away!

6. Arrange the carrots and radishes
in rows around the edge of a large
plate or platter.

7. Place a small bowl in the center
of the platter and fill it with dip.

The Spring Will Come Box

MINI SPRING BULBS

Types to Try

Imagine how exciting it will be to see the first flowers of spring right outside your window. If you plant a variety of bulbs, you will have flowers in bloom for four to six weeks in early spring.

CROCUS ~ *Crocus*

STRIPED BEAUTY grows to be 4 to 6 inches tall and has white flowers with purple stripes.

ADVANCE grows to be 4 to 6 inches tall and has flowers that are yellow on the inside and shades of purple on the outside.

DAFFODIL ~ *Narcissus*

LITTLE GEM grows to be 3 to 6 inches tall and has yellow flowers.

JACK SNIPE grows to be 12 inches tall and has white flowers with yellow centers.

ANGEL'S TEARS grows to be 7 inches tall and has white flowers.

IRIS ~ *Iris reticulata*

PURPLE GEM grows to be 4 inches tall and has deep purple flowers.

JOYCE grows to be 4 to 6 inches tall and has flowers in sky blue and gold.

GRAPE HYACINTH ~ *Muscari*

BLUE SPIKE grows to be 6 inches tall and has tiny purple cone-shaped flowers.

Planting

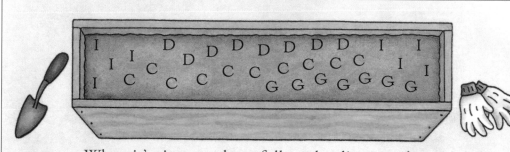

When it's time to plant, follow the diagram above.
The letters in the window box show you where to plant the bulbs.

C is for CROCUS   I is for IRIS

D is for DAFFODIL   G is for GRAPE HYACINTH

Crocus, iris, daffodil, and grape hyacinth bulbs can be planted from October through mid-November. They should be 2 to 3 inches apart and 3 to 6 inches deep. Plant with the pointed ends up. Bulbs should be at least 2 inches from the edge of the window box. They will have better protection against freezing temperatures if they have more soil around them.

Green shoots may begin to appear in the fall, but when the cold weather arrives the bulbs will stop growing until spring. They must have a cold period of at least 6 weeks. Flowers will bloom in March and April.

You can plant bulbs indoors in February, but they must be stored in the refrigerator for 8 to 16 weeks before they are planted. Wrap the bulbs in paper bags rather than plastic bags to prevent them from rotting while they are being stored.

Picture This

Painting a picture of your flowers is a way to make sure their beauty will not be forgotten. Famous artists such as Monet and Renoir painted theirs and because they did we can still enjoy their gardens today.

A Tiny Centerpiece

To make a tiny centerpiece you will need:

Jelly jars or jam jars
Perfume bottles

1. Look around your house to find empty jars or bottles that would make good miniature vases for flowers. Always ask permission, especially if the bottles or jars are not quite empty.

2. Wash them well, and fill them half way with water.

make a dollhouse bouquet

3. Cut flowers from your window box and arrange them in the tiny jars and bottles.

4. Now you can decorate your table with a pretty springtime centerpiece. Or you may want to make a tiny bouquet to put on a tiny table in your doll's house.

paint a picture for yourself and one for a doll

Painting a Still Life

Now that you have a centerpiece you can create a masterpiece by painting a still life of your flowers. Why not paint a miniature picture for your doll's house as well?

Over the Winter

Depending on how cold the winters are where you live, there may be certain months of the year when it is not possible to grow a garden in your window box. But you can still be a gardener. Here are some ideas to keep your garden growing over the winter.

PAPER WHITES
Narcissi 'Galilee'

Paper whites are bulbs that can be forced to bloom indoors. Each bulb has a dormant plant inside waiting for the right combination of moisture and light to grow. The blossoms are like perfume. They can make an entire room smell sweet. To grow paper whites you will need:

> *1 bowl or pot, 4 to 6 inches deep*
> *6 to 10 paper white bulbs*
> *Gravel or small rocks*

1. Fill the bowl or pot with 1½ to 2 inches of rocks or gravel, then pour in just enough water so that the rocks and gravel are covered.

2. Place the paper white bulbs on top of the rocks or gravel with the pointed ends up.

3. Watch closely over the next few days. You will see roots forming and growing from the bulbs down into the rocks or gravel.

4. Now place the bowl in a sunny window, away from any direct heat from a heater.

5. The water level will drop each day. As it does, add just enough to cover the rocks and gravel, but be careful not to add too much. If the water covers the bulbs, it may cause them to rot.

6. After a couple of weeks, leaves will grow, and after about six weeks your paper whites will flower.

if the stems droop tie them with a ribbon

Sometimes paper whites grow so tall that they begin to flop or droop. You can tie a ribbon around the stems to keep them upright.

HEAD FULL OF GRASS
Triticum vulgare

To grow a head full of grass you will need:

> *White paper cups*
> *Potting soil*
> *Wheat grass seeds*
> *Markers or crayons*

1. Soak the wheat grass seeds in warm water overnight.

2. Make a small hole in the bottom of each cup so that the excess water can drain out, and put a tray under the cups to protect your table.

3. With crayons or markers, draw a face on each of the paper cups.

4. Fill the cups with soil, leaving 1/2 inch of space at the top.

5. Spread a single layer of seeds over the surface of the soil, and cover them with 1/4 inch of soil.

6. Add water as needed each day to keep the soil moist, but not soggy.

7. In five to seven days, you will see green grass hair growing on the top of your paper cup heads.

Beware: If you happen to have a cat in the house, you may find that your grass is being nibbled. Wheat grass is a favorite among cats.

ORANGE TREE
Citrus sinensis

If you save the seeds from oranges you have eaten, you can grow your own orange tree. You will need:

> *Orange seeds*
> *Potting soil*
> *6 inch pot with drainage hole*
> *Gravel or perlite*
> *Fertilizer*

1. Put 1 to 2 inches of perlite or gravel in the bottom of your pot and then fill it to within 1 inch of the top with potting soil.

2. Water the soil well and fertilize it with liquid fertilizer.

3. Plant the orange seeds 3 inches apart and 1/2 inch deep.

4. Place the pot near a warm, sunny window and keep the soil moist, but not soggy.

5. After 14 to 21 days, when the seeds have sprouted, remove all except the strongest seedling.

6. Fertilize once a month, except between October and February, when it's best not to fertilize at all.

7. Move your orange tree outdoors during warm weather, but be sure to give it plenty of water on hot days. Move it back indoors again in early September and keep it in a cool, sunny spot, away from heaters, over the winter.

You can plant orange seeds any time of year, but it's best to plant them in December or January so they will be ready for spring, when they do most of their growing. In a few years, you may be eating your own home-grown oranges.

Things to Do

Along with the planting instructions for the window box gardens in the first part of this book, you will find a page of activities or recipes to follow using the plants you have grown. Here are a few more ideas you can try.

The Hungry Rabbit Box
SALAD DRESSING
continued from page 23

Once you've made a salad with the greens from your window box, you can dress it up with tangy vinegar and oil dressing. You will need:

chop the herbs

toss gently

¼ cup olive oil or vegetable oil
2 tablespoons vinegar or
*   lemon juice*
½ teaspoon fresh or dried herbs
¼ teaspoon mustard
Salt and pepper to taste

1. Combine the ingredients in a jar with a tight fitting lid.

2. Shake it well, pour it over your salad, and toss gently with a fork.

The Candy Box
FLOWERS FOR SALAD
continued from page 27

The marigolds, nasturtiums, and pansies from your window box will dress up a salad with their colorful petals. Use the whole flower or the individual petals. Nasturtiums have a slightly peppery taste and signet marigolds have a mild citrus flavor. Pansies are pretty to look at, but they have a bland taste.

Always ask an adult to help identify flowers before you use them. Never use flowers that have been sprayed with insecticides.

The Tea Party Box
SUNSHINE TEA
continued from page 31

To make a pitcher of sunshine tea, you will need:

Mint or lemon balm leaves

1. Wash the leaves, pile them loosely in a clear glass container, and fill it to the top with water.

invite your friends to tea

Please Come

2. Leave the container in the sun for several hours. The longer your

tea stays in the sun, the stronger the flavor will be.

3. Strain out the leaves and then transfer the tea into a pitcher.

4. Now fill some glasses with ice cubes, and pour the tea.

The Pizza Box
GARLIC BRAIDS
continued from page 43

braid the garlic leaves

tie ends with a ribbon

To make a garlic braid you will need:

3 garlic bulbs with leaves attached
1 piece of ribbon, 12 inches long

1. Harvest 3 ripe garlic bulbs and braid the leaves together, beginning at the tops of the bulbs.

2. Use the ribbon to tie a bow around the ends, and hang your garlic braid on the kitchen wall as an edible decoration!

The Sweet & Sour Box
SWEET PICKLES
continued from page 39

To make sweet pickles you will need:

1 quart-size container with a lid
5 cups cucumbers, sliced into
* ¹/₄ inch rounds*
³/₄ cup sugar
2 tablespoons salt
1 small onion, thinly sliced
¹/₂ cup cider vinegar
1 quart water
1 to 2 tablespoons celery seeds

1. Combine the celery seed, onions, cucumbers, and salt in a bowl. Allow the mixture to rest for one hour, then drain off excess liquid.

2. Place the cucumber mix in the jar, leaving one inch of space at the top.

3. In a large saucepan, mix the sugar, water, and vinegar together. Bring to a boil and stir for 2 to 3 minutes, until the sugar dissolves.

4. Pour the liquid into the jar to cover the cucumbers. Cool to room temperature, then refrigerate. Eat the pickles the next day or you can refrigerate them for up to one week.

The Everlasting Box
ARRANGING FLOWERS
continued from page 51

To make a gift basket you will need:

Dried statice, Chinese lanterns,
* and money plant*
1 small or medium sized basket
1 piece of ribbon, 18 inches long
A block of florist's foam

stick stems into florist's foam

decorate the basket with a ribbon

1. Cut a piece of florist's foam to fit the bottom of your basket.

2. Push the stems of your flowers into the foam, varying the lengths to make a nice arrangement.

3. Place the foam and flowers in the basket and tie on a ribbon.

Through the Year

You can plant more than one type of window box within a year. If you begin with lettuce in early spring, you then can plant flowers for summer, and in late autumn, bulbs to bloom the following spring. Here are four combinations to try.

EARLY SPRING
Hungry Rabbit Box

LATE SPRING
Bouquet Box

AUTUMN
Spring Will Come Box

LATE SPRING
Sweet & Sour Box

AUTUMN
Spring Will Come Box

EARLY SPRING
Hungry Rabbit Box

LATE SPRING
Jack Be Little Box

EARLY SPRING
Candy Box

LATE SUMMER
Baby Veggie Box

AUTUMN
Spring Will Come Box

Keeping a Journal

Gardeners keep journals to help them remember to do important things throughout the year. Certain months are good for certain garden activities. Your journal will be filled with your own thoughts and ideas, but here are some of the things you might do from month to month.

JANUARY
decide which window box gardens to plant this year

FEBRUARY
buy seeds and bulbs from catalogs or the garden center

MARCH
plant cool weather plants like pansies and mixed greens

APRIL
eagerly await the blooming of bulbs planted in autumn

MAY
harvest mixed greens, plant seeds for flowers in summer

JUNE
water frequently, pick pansies, pull out weeds

JULY
keep watering, pick mint leaves, make sunshine tea

AUGUST
plant baby veggies for autumn harvest, pickle cucumbers

SEPTEMBER
harvest oregano, basil, and garlic, make pizza sauce

OCTOBER
harvest pumpkins, plant bulbs for flowers in spring

NOVEMBER
catch up on garden journal, plant paper whites indoors

DECEMBER
order seed and bulb catalogs, plant an orange tree

You can use the charts and logs on the following pages to keep records about planting, watering, garden expenses, special visitors, and interesting things you may notice happening in and around your window box.

Keeping a Planting Log

A planting log is a chart that gardeners use for
keeping track of when seeds or bulbs are planted, when they
sprout, when the flowers bloom, and when the herbs and vegetables
are ready to harvest. The example below shows how to use the
planting logs provided on the following pages.

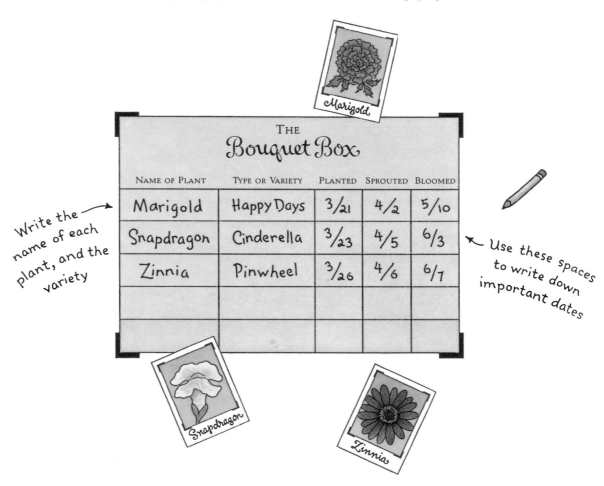

Write the name of each plant, and the variety

THE
Bouquet Box

Name of Plant	Type or Variety	Planted	Sprouted	Bloomed
Marigold	Happy Days	3/21	4/2	5/10
Snapdragon	Cinderella	3/23	4/5	6/3
Zinnia	Pinwheel	3/26	4/6	6/7

Use these spaces to write down important dates

If you use a light pencil, you will be able to erase
the logs at the end of the growing season and use them again the
next time you plant. Or you can save your records and compare
how your garden grows from one year to the next.

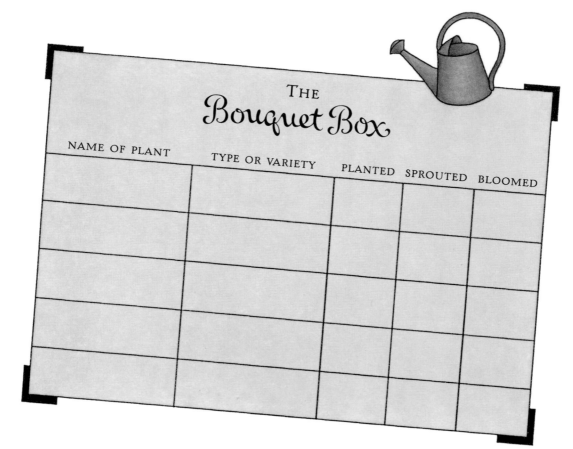

THE
Bouquet Box

NAME OF PLANT	TYPE OR VARIETY	PLANTED	SPROUTED	BLOOMED

THE
Shady Lane Box

NAME OF PLANT	TYPE OR VARIETY	PLANTED	SPROUTED	BLOOMED

THE
Hungry Rabbit Box

NAME OF PLANT	TYPE OR VARIETY	PLANTED	SPROUTED	HARVESTED

THE
Candy Box

NAME OF PLANT	TYPE OR VARIETY	PLANTED	SPROUTED	BLOOMED

The Tea Party Box

NAME OF PLANT	TYPE OR VARIETY	PLANTED	SPROUTED	BLOOMED

The Night & Day Box

NAME OF PLANT	TYPE OR VARIETY	PLANTED	SPROUTED	BLOOMED

THE
Sweet & Sour Box

NAME OF PLANT	TYPE OR VARIETY	PLANTED	SPROUTED	HARVESTED

THE
Pizza Box

NAME OF PLANT	TYPE OR VARIETY	PLANTED	SPROUTED	HARVESTED

THE
Jack Be Little Box

NAME OF PLANT	TYPE OR VARIETY	PLANTED	SPROUTED	HARVESTED

THE
Everlasting Box

NAME OF PLANT	TYPE OR VARIETY	PLANTED	SPROUTED	COLLECTED

THE
Baby Veggie Box

NAME OF PLANT	TYPE OR VARIETY	PLANTED	SPROUTED	HARVESTED

THE
Spring Will Come Box

NAME OF PLANT	TYPE OR VARIETY	PLANTED	SPROUTED	BLOOMED

Keeping a Watering Log

After you have planted your seeds and bulbs, it is very important to keep your garden watered. The watering logs on the following pages will help you remember when to water. You can use the same logs to keep a record of when you fertilize.

Begin by filling in the numbers for each day of the month. Because the numbers will fall on different days of the week each year, you may want to use a light pencil. That way you can gently erase your marks at the end of the year, and use the watering logs again.

MARCH

SUN	MON	TUE	WED	THU	FRI	SAT
		1 W	2	3	4	5 W
6	7 F	8	9 W	10	11	12
13 W	14	15	16	17 W	18	19
20	21 W	22	23	24	25 W	26 F
27	28	29 W	30	31		

Write in the number for each day of the month →

Mark the letter "W" on the days when you water ←

Mark the letter "F" on the days when you fertilize ←

If you and your family plan to take a trip, be sure to find someone to tend your garden. Explain your watering logs to a friend or neighbor and ask them to water and fertilize for you while you are away.

When you come home again, you can say thank you by offering to share your flowers and vegetables.

Mark the calendar each time

JANUARY

SUN	MON	TUE	WED	THU	FRI	SAT

Mark W when you water

FEBRUARY

SUN	MON	TUE	WED	THU	FRI	SAT

MARCH

SUN	MON	TUE	WED	THU	FRI	SAT

and each

you water

Mark F when you fertilize

time you fertilize

Mark the calendar each time

JULY

SUN	MON	TUE	WED	THU	FRI	SAT

Mark W when you water

AUGUST

SUN	MON	TUE	WED	THU	FRI	SAT

SEPTEMBER

SUN	MON	TUE	WED	THU	FRI	SAT

and each

you water

Mark F when you fertilize

time you fertilize

If you do not live near a garden center where you can buy seeds and bulbs, you can order them through the mail. Look on the back pages of gardening magazines at your library to find the names and addresses of seed and bulb companies.

SEED COMPANIES

Name_____

Address_____

City_____

State_____Zip Code_____

Telephone_____

Name_____

Address_____

City_____

State_____Zip Code_____

Telephone_____

Name_____

Address_____

City_____

State_____Zip Code_____

Telephone_____

BULB COMPANIES

Name_____

Address_____

City_____

State_____Zip Code_____

Telephone_____

Name_____

Address_____

City_____

State_____Zip Code_____

Telephone_____

Name_____

Address_____

City_____

State_____Zip Code_____

Telephone_____

During the winter months, when it's too cold to garden, you can look through the pages of your catalogs and decide which seeds and bulbs to order for the coming year.

PURCHASE LOG

Keep a careful record of how much you spend and what you buy.

DATE	SUPPLIER	ITEM	QUANTITY	COST

Who visited my window box

INSECTS

BIRDS

insects.

garden…

BUTTERFLIES

_____

_____

_____

_____

_____

FRIENDS

_____

_____

_____

_____

_____

birds, butterflies & friends

Favorite Plants

The plants in your window box may come and go
with the seasons, but that doesn't mean they will be forgotten.
If you grow a marigold that is too beautiful for words,
you can always save it in a picture.

Use these pages to draw or paint your favorite plants,
or you can glue or tape photographs or pressed flowers onto
the pages. Like a botanist, be sure to write the name of
each plant on the line at the bottom of the box.

Things I want to remember...

How did your garden grow?
What did you like best? What will you try next time?

_____

_____

_____

_____

_____

_____

_____

_____

_____

_____

_____

You must wait for the time until the blossom of roses comes

ink

What did you discover that might be helpful
when you plant your window box garden next year?

_____

_____

_____

_____

_____

_____

_____

_____

_____

_____

_____

... for my garden next year

about the author

KAREN FAUSCH

received her degree in Fine Arts from New York University.
She then studied horticulture and landscape design at The New York
Botanical Garden, where she taught in the children's gardening program.
She currently works as a landscape designer in New York City.

about the illustrator

LAURA JANE COATS

studied Fine Arts at the University of California.
An author and illustrator of several books for children,
she has a studio in Larkspur, California.